seven
bad
cats

Moe Bonneau

sourcebooks
jabberwocky

Today I put on
my boots and my coat,
and seven bad cats
jumped into my boat.

There was one bad cat
who ate from my traps,

and two bad cats
on my oars, taking naps.

Three bad cats
teasing crabs from above,
and four bad cats
who kept stealing my gloves.

There were five bad cats
who shredded the sails,

and six bad cats
getting sick in my pail.

There were seven bad cats
who flipped over my ship,
and eight flying mates
not keen for a dip!

There were cats overboard!
Cats in dismay!

Cats clinging to cats!
Cats swimming astray!

I splished and I splashed,
but all seemed very grim,

for I am one sailor
who does not know how to swim!

Slowly I sank,
only fish by my side,

when out of the deep
I started to rise...

Fourteen small paws
lifted me in their grip,

and seven good cats
rescued me to my ship!

There were six good cats
who rowed with their tails.

And five good cats
collecting clams as we sailed.

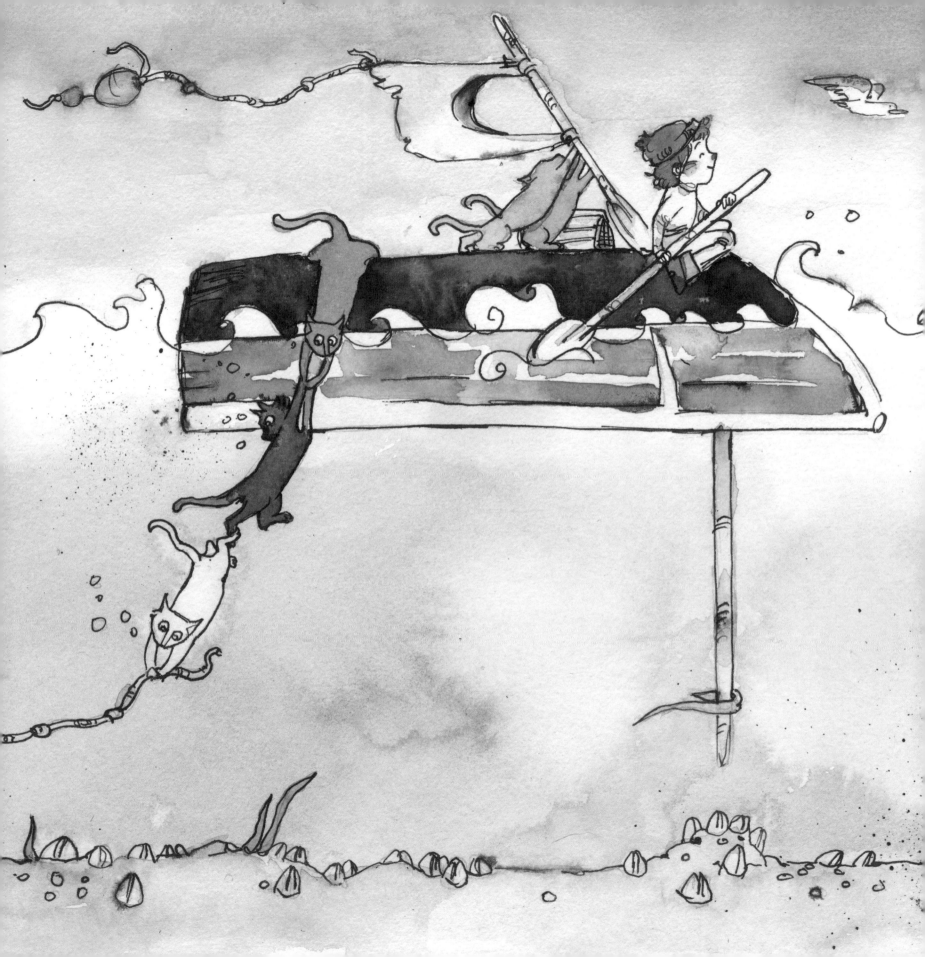

There were four good cats
who pulled and who shoved,

and three good cats
cooking dinner with love.

There were two good cats
who sang as I clapped.

And one good cat
warming up my cold lap.

Tonight I take off
my boots and my coat,
with seven bad cats
asleep in my boat.

For two very bad cats, Winnie and Chicken.
—M.B.

Published by Sourcebooks Jabberwocky, an imprint of Sourcebooks, Inc.
P.O. Box 4410, Naperville, Illinois 60567-4410
(630) 961-3900
Fax: (630) 961-2168
sourcebooks.com

Library of Congress Cataloging-in-Publication Data is on file with the publisher.

Source of Production: Leo Paper, Heshan City, Guangdong Province, China
Date of Production: March 2018
Run Number: 5011529

Printed and bound in China.
LEO 10 9 8 7 6 5 4 3 2 1